Harry Coghill

Oak and Maple

English and Canadian Verses

Harry Coghill

Oak and Maple
English and Canadian Verses

ISBN/EAN: 9783337190125

Printed in Europe, USA, Canada, Australia, Japan

Cover: Foto ©Andreas Hilbeck / pixelio.de

More available books at **www.hansebooks.com**

OAK AND MAPLE

ENGLISH AND CANADIAN VERSES

BY

MRS. H. COGHILL

(Annie L. Walker)

Author of " Plays for Children," " Against Her Will,"
" Lady's Holm," &c., &c.

LONDON

KEGAN PAUL, TRENCH, TRÜBNER & CO. Ltd.

1890

TO THE DEAR MEMORY
OF MY MOTHER
I DEDICATE THESE VERSES,
CHIEFLY WRITTEN FOR HER PLEASURE

PREFACE.

I CANNOT let this little book go out into the world without a word of apology for offering so slight an object to the public notice. This, then, is what I have to say for myself:

Many years ago, when I was yet in my teens, the larger proportion of these verses were written and printed. They were written in the Canadian back-woods, and were first published in a collected form in Montreal. But, both before and after the gathering of them into a little volume, various single sets of verses (I will not use the word "poems,") found their way into Canadian newspapers and magazines, and thence into American ones. Books were in those days rarely produced in Canada, and mine found many and kind readers, and made a little success.

But I returned to England. Cares and anxieties, and the swiftly-accomplished loss of all those who had had pleasure in my doings, had swept the book and its contents almost out of my mind, when I was startled one day by seeing some verses of my own printed among those to be sung at a great temper-ance meeting. I asked whence they came, and was told "from Moody and Sankey's Hymn-book." I borrowed a copy of Messrs. Moody and Sankey's collection, and there, slightly altered, set to a tune which is not, certainly, strikingly beautiful, and attributed to somebody I never heard of, were my poor verses, beginning, " Work, for the night is coming."

In later editions of this collection my name is inserted, but the alterations are retained (indeed, without them the tune would not fit) : and though it is just possible, however unlikely, that an author may have some claim for copyright, the editors have never in any way communicated with me. The same verses are now to be found in a good many other hymn-books, and some others are wandering about in print. I am glad it should be so, but I am not glad that they should appear in a garbled form, or with somebody else's name appended. Nor do I like to be told, as I was by one collector when I modestly prayed him to print the words as I wrote them, that a hymn was not the property of its inventor, but of " the Church ! " The poor little " hymn " in question was not worth a fuss—yet one has a kind of parental feeling for one's children, even if they are small and shy; and that I may gather mine together and let them claim their true parentage is my chief reason and excuse for once more venturing into the world of writers and readers. A. L. C.

COGHURST, *September*, 1890.

INDEX.

INDEX.

POEMS.

A LAMENT FOR BOOKS.

I WISH some wise magician
Would clear from my puzzled brain
A question I often ponder,
And always ponder in vain.

Why, I should like to ask him,
Are there no such books to-day
As those that possessed our childhood.
And ruled us with exquisite sway ?

In the quiet Winter evenings,
With the new book on one's knee,
And a soul wrapt away in its pages,
What bliss there used to be !

Or out in the Summer garden
With some song of joy or pain
Flooding one's heart with its music—
Oh, could *that* come back again !

B

Is the world more flippant and duller?
Are the stars gone out of the sky?
Or is it that, as we grow older,
We grow praisers of days gone by?

Are the giants gone, and have pigmies
Begun to wield the pen?
Or are we so sadly wiser
That we judge where we worshipped then?

We sip our tea and gossip
As we lounge in an easy chair,
And—just for something to talk of -
The last new book is there.

" These tales of adventure are thrilling;
One gets so excited, you see;
But he surely does too much killing—-
Do you like this Indian tea?

" And that other book—so well written !
Such amazing fertility, too,
It must be his sixtieth volume;
I think 'tis too much, don't you?"

Oh, where are the books of our childhood,
The books we loved so well?
Is it we who are changed? or the writers?
I wish some wise man could tell!

LOVE.

CHILD of the everlasting love,
　　Sweet inmate of our world of pain,
By thee life's deepest pulses move,
　　From thee our souls new courage gain ;
With varying aspect, steadfast mind,
Thee ever by our path we find.

A freakish boy on youth and maid
　　A thousand tricks thou'rt wont to try,
Through calm and storm, through sun and shade,
　　Beside their pathway thou dost fly—
The sweetest semblance of a guide
That ever mortal pilgrim tried.

Or onward, where the matron staid
　　Paces beside her anxious mate,
In new and sober garb arrayed,
　　Thou walk'st along with step sedate ;
Thy ready hand and sunny smile
The burden of their day beguile.

And age goes creeping on its way,
　　A grey-haired spouse, a tottering dame—
Changed is their world, and changed are they;
　　Thou, only thou, art still the same :
Youth's joy, life's solace, age's friend,
Heaven's self thy mission shall not end.

JOY IN PILGRIMAGE.

PILGRIM, that passest by this narrow road,
Dost thou go silent, sorrowing all the day?
Consider, was it joyance that did stay
Thy feet when they more swiftly might have trod?
Lift up thy heart in thankful praise to God!
For He, who bade thee take a rugged way,
Hath given thee strength and guidance, and the ray
Of Heaven's pure light to cheer thee, and hath showed
A golden crown that waits thee at the end.
Rejoice! it is thy heritage—rejoice!
Go ever with thanksgiving in thy heart;
So shall thy worship to His throne ascend;
So shall thy soul grow purer, and thy voice
Learn in the angels' songs to bear a part.

SONG OF THE WILLOW.

" Willow, pale willow, I pray thee tell
  What yestereve in thy shade befell?"

" Yestereve, when the west was red,
  A woman came with hurried tread.

" Awhile she stood on the river's brink,
  Waiting, methought, for the sun to sink.

" She looked on the waters, dark and deep ;
  ' This cradle,' she whispered, ' shall rock me to sleep.

" ' Oh, river, lone river, hide me, I pray ;
  Hide me well from the curious day.

" ' Wrap me in weeds and hold me tight ;
  Hide me for ever in shadow and night.'

" A spring from the shore, an eddy below—
  Silent as ever the waters flow."

" Willow, pale willow, the night was fair —
  It told no story of pain or care!"

" The night was fair, and the moonbeams fell,
 Silvery and soft, on the river's swell.

" A boat upset came down with the tide,
 All night long I saw naught beside.

" I saw it before, when the rowers sang,
 And over the water their laughter rang.

" Last night I saw it drifting alone—
 Where were the joyous rowers gone ? "

" Willow, pale willow, the morn is bright ;
 Such tales as these are for eve and night."

" Ask me no more—there are pleasant hills
 And meadows fair that the sunlight fills ;

" Here the shadows but change their form,
 Flitting, yet lingering, night and morn.

" Sorrow and death—I see them still ;
 Pain, and all phantoms of human ill.

" Bones at my deep roots mouldering lie—
 Ask me no more of my history ! "

A THANKSGIVING.

For those departed this life in Thy faith and fear.

FATHER, we bless Thee for the cherished dead,
  The lost whom Thou hast gathered to Thy fold·
Though when we parted clouds were overhead,
    And Death's dark river round their pathway rolled,
        Yet they are safe—and we
    Do bless Thee for their blest eternity.

E'en while we linger with a long regret
  By the low grassy mound, some loved one's bed,
Our hearts soar upward till we half forget
    The bitter moment when that couch was spread,
        Seeing the golden street,
    And listening for the tread of angel feet.

Or when we lose awhile that vision blest,
  Taking the burden of our daily care,
Still does the memory of our dear ones' rest
    Come with the toil that they no longer share ;
        They do not weep,
    But wake in smiles who wept themselves to sleep.

This thought goes with us through the busy day—
    And in the silent watches of the night,
In weary wakeful hours we gladly say,
    " They evermore behold th' unclouded light,
        This dark and troubled scene
    Remembering, yet as though it ne'er had been."

Thus, o'er the shadowy pathway that we tread,
    They from Thy heaven can cast a sunbeam still,
That Love, though linked with those we call the dead,
    The mission Thou hast given may yet fulfil,
        Teaching our hearts to guess
    The greater Love, even Thine, by ours, the less.

THE SWALLOW.

One having built its nest in our church.

THUS hath the swallow found
Close by Thine altar, Lord, her place of rest,
Hither she hasteth when, with wearied breast,
 She ends her daily round.

Thou, whose benignant care
Still loves to guard Thy smallest creature well,
Dost smile as pleased to see her fearless dwell
 Where holiest precincts are.

So from a world of ill,
With trouble-laden hearts and sad, we fly,
And fain beneath Thy roof, beneath Thine eye,
 Would have our dwelling still.

But thus it may not be—
A thousand voices call us back again,
A thousand ties of love, of hope, of pain,
 Drag us away from Thee.

Oh, that beyond the height
Of any tide on Time's tumultuous sea,
Thy wearied ones were harboured safe with Thee,
Fearing nor storm nor night !

Or that like her, whose nest
Thy walls surround, and with it all her love,
No daily task may us too far remove
To come to Thee for rest !

OLD LETTERS.

I CANNOT touch them with a careless hand,
  I cannot view them with a careless eye ;
Their spells the shades of love and youth command,
  And bind the present to the days gone by.

I touch them with a reverent hand, and see !
  What shadowy forms around me seem to rise ;
Gentle and fair, and oh, how dear to me
  Are those familiar forms, those friendly eyes !

Again return the hours without a cloud,
  When perfect bliss seemed possible on earth,
Those hours before the child's glad spirit bowed
  To learn joy's emptiness and sorrow's worth.

Some word that, once familiar to my ear,
  Now long unheard, brings back the speaker's tone—
Some name that silent memory still holds dear—
  These breathe to me, these still can make my own.

And of the dreams all human hearts must weave
  The hopes and fears, the springs of joy or pain—
(Ghosts that Time lays, no more to glad or grieve)—
  How many only on these leaves remain !

Yet, though the keener feelings of the time
  When first they spoke from heart to heart be gone ;
Though hushed the funeral knell, the bridal chime,
  And guest or mourner wends his way alone :

Yet must the charm, which still has power to bring
  The faintest reflex of a past once bright,
Be sweet as are the evening tints that fling
  Memories of sunshine o'er the scene they light.

PRECIOUS HOURS.

TREASURE the hour of joy—
Welcome each draught of bliss, each golden dream :
Find, if thou canst, beside life's rapid stream,
    Pleasures without alloy ;
But ever let thy heart's deep homage be,
Amid thy gladness, His, who gave it thee.

Treasure the time of grief—
Weep if thou wilt, but in that darker day
The humbled spirit sweetly learns to say,
    "God giveth glad relief ; "
And sorrow dearer far than joy shall be,
If it but bring thy God more near to thee.

Treasure the hour of prayer—
There, seek from God food for thy hungry soul,
Full, and rich store ; no scant, penurious dole
    Shall ever meet thee there.
Put by earth's sparkling cup of false delight,
And drink from Heaven's own chalice life and light.

SPRING AND AUTUMN.

"A little dust to overweep."

—MRS. BROWNING.

UTTERLY, utterly out of our life,
    Already each trace of his life is gone ;
Only sometimes, in the quiet eve,
    We stand, with a sigh, by the sculptured stone,
Which tells us the form we used to greet,
Dust amid dust, lies low at our feet.

Bright came the Spring with sun and shower,
    The wood paths smiled in their vernal green ;
To-day we have trodden the emerald grass,
    And wandered beneath the leafy screen ;---
He welcomed the Summer's early bloom,—
Now, it can only brighten his tomb.

Sigh, O leaves, on your rustling boughs ;
    Even amid your smiling, sigh !
Did he not love your changeful charms ?
    Yet, 'mid them all, he lay down to die
Ye, in beauty, survive to-day,
A little while, ere ye pass away.

The snow will come, and, with silvery veil,
    Wrap the earth for its Winter's rest ;
Before the flowers of the Spring awake,
    We, like him, may sleep on its breast.
Time will each beauty of Spring restore :
Only life's flowers return no more.

THE NIGHT COMETH.

WORK! for the night is coming;
  Work! through the morning hours :
Work! while the dew is sparkling;
  Work! 'mid the springing flowers;
Work ! while the day grows brighter,
  Under the glowing sun ;
Work! for the night is coming,—
  Night, when man's work is done.

Work ! for the night is coming ;
  Work! through the sunny noon ;
Fill the bright hours with labour,
  Rest cometh sure and soon.
Give to each flying minute
  Something to keep in store ;
Work ! for the night is coming,—
  Night, when man works no more.

Work ! for the night is coming ;
  Under the sunset skies,
While their bright tints are glowing,
  Work ! for the daylight flies ;

C

Work ! till the last beam fadeth,
  Fadeth to shine no more ;
Work ! while the night is darkening,—
  Night, when man's work is o'er.

THE DYING SUMMER.

GENTLY, sadly the Summer is dying—
   Under the shivering, trembling boughs,
With a low soft moan, the breeze is flying ;
The breeze, that was once so fresh and sweet,
Is passing as swift as Time's hurrying feet,
And where the withered roses are lying,
The beautiful Summer is surely dying.

Gently, sadly the waves are sighing,
   The leaves are mourning that they must fall ;
And the plaintive waters keep replying ;
They miss the light that has decked them long,
They have caught the last bird's farewell song,
And lowly they murmur, from day to day,
"The beautiful Summer is passing away."

Gently, sadly the moon reclining
   High on her throne of azure and gold,
With wan clear light, o'er the world is shining ;
Wherever she turns there are teardrops shed,
Such as we give to the cherished dead ;
They will gleam till the chilly morn is breaking,
And the flowers with their last pale smiles are waking.

Wildly, sadly the night wind, swelling,
   Chants a measure weird and strange;
Hark ! of the coming storm he is telling,
And the trembling life, that was almost gone,
Flickers and shrinks at the dreaded tone,
And scarcely lingers where, lowly lying,
The tender and beautiful Summer is dying.

EVENING TIME.

" AT evening time there shall be light."
    Yes, when old age shall come,
  And night's dark shades obscure the path,
    Whereon we're travelling home ;
  When, 'wildered by the gathering gloom,
    Appalling fears arise,
  The first pure gleams of heavenly light
    Shall brighten all the skies.

" At evening time there shall be light."
    If sorrow's hand should bear
  Cold on our hearts, and draw her shroud
    O'er what we hold most dear ;
  Though sunshine, with each charm it brings,
    May seem for ever fled ;
  Light, from Heaven's own celestial springs,
    Shall rest upon our head.

" At evening time there shall be light."
    Oh ! promise ever sweet
  To those who tread an unknown way,
    With faint and faltering feet ;

They need not fear the coming hours
    When sunset shall be past,
Since One who knows the pathway well
    Has promised light at last.

THE BRIDAL.

Weave the garlands bright and gay,
 For the bride, to-morrow;
Raise the festal arches high,
 For the bride, to-morrow;
Deck the church with laurel boughs,
Seek the myrtle where it grows,
Lilies, for the sunny brows
 Round the bride, to-morrow.

See! they fade, the flowers ye bring,
 For the bride, to-morrow;
Little fragrance they shall fling
 Round the bride, to-morrow;
Cast them forth, and bring, instead,
Yew, that mourneth for the dead,
Twine dark ivy overhead,
 For the bride, to-morrow.

Useless all your care shall be,
 For the bride, to-morrow;
He, the bridegroom that hath wooed,
 Stays not for to-morrow;

'Neath his kiss her lips grow pale,
And her fluttering pulses fail;
Loud and deep shall be the wail
    Round her grave to-morrow.

WEDDED AND WIDOWED.

HER hand is clasped in his, the words
　　That bind till death are calmly said,
Although they know that Azrael's wing
　　Is closely hovering o'er his head.

In happy eyes at bridal hour
　　The tears of love have softly shone ;
But hers await the coming day
　　Of widowhood, when he is gone.

" As long as both shall live "—but see !
　　The term is ending even now,
Had not her heart interpreted,
　　With fuller scope, its solemn vow.

Full flows the life-blood through her veins,
　　The meadows long shall know her tread ;
Yet she is vowed for all her days,
　　Vowed to the memory of the dead !

The rite is done.　Her pallid cheek
　　Knows not the dawn of bridal blush,
Hearing the sacred name of wife
　　Steal through the darkened chamber's hush.

The bridegroom's kiss is on her lips,
  Strange sweet !   At once the first and last.
Love's chalice held one slender draught
  Scarce drained before the spirit passed.

SEEKING.

"Why is this stupendous intelligence so retired and silent, while present in all the scenes of the earth, and in all the paths and abodes of men?"

—FOSTER.

WHERE dost Thou dwell,
Unknown, unseen, yet knowing, seeing all?
We find Thee not in hermit's lonely cell,
 Nor lofty palace hall.

No more at eve
Thy form is with us on the dusty road;
The dead sleep on, though loving hearts may grieve;
 The suffering bear their load.

Night closes round—
In the green forest aisles no leaf is stirred;
So hushed, as if Heaven's distant music-sound
 Might even here be heard.

Through all we see,
Up to the azure roof with stars inwrought,
Through all Earth's temple, do we look for Thee;
 Alas! we find Thee not.

Yet, Thou art near;
Father! forgive our weak and failing sight;
Forgive, and make our darkness noonday clear
With Thy celestial light.

Or, if it please Thee best
That we, unseeing, wander on our way,
Then in the darkness let us find our rest,
And wait till Heaven for day.

SUMMER HYMN.

HARK! Earth begins her matin hymn;
    The wide expanse of hill and plain,
The river, and the mountain breeze,
    Uniting, swell the glad refrain;
Day, throned upon the eastern heights,
    From herb and flower bids incense rise
To mingle in the azure heaven,
    With Nature's wordless harmonics.

All things—the insect world around,
    The squirrels peeping from the shade,
The birds that warble on the boughs,
    The herds amid the sunshine laid;
All living things, and all beside,
    Thy works, whate'er their form may be,
Varied by Thy creating hand,
    Are one, O God, in praising Thee.

Nor, Father! let Thy latest born,
    The chosen object of Thy care,
Contemn the universal hymn
    That Nature raises everywhere.

For blessings of the opening year,
    For Spring and Summer's sunny days,
And for the harvest's promised store,
    Accept, O Lord, our grateful praise.

THE LAND OF REST.

Where art thou, land of rest?
    Oft, amid evening skies,
Rich outlines, as of dwellings blest,
    Before my vision rise ;
But ah ! they fade as night draws on ;
They fade, they pale, as sinks the sun.

When morning beams are bright,
    The distant mountain slopes,
All bathed in soft and tender light,
    Seem fair as youth's fond hopes :
But noon must steal their brave array,
And leave them cold, and stern, and gray.

Oh distant, yet beloved ;
    Art thou, that seem'st so fair,
Naught but a poet's fancy vain,
    A phantom of the air ?
Never to bless the longing sight,
With all thy fulness of delight ?

What though in passing dream,
    The weary tread thy shore,

Bathe in thy river's tranquil stream,
   And learn thy sacred lore,
Day calls them back, to meet again
Their daily toil, their daily pain.

MORNING.

Morning ! whose earliest, purest ray
    Sheds beauty on the distant hills,
And whose light winds the tree-tops sway
    Above the newly wakened rills,
Many a bright floweret opens to thy smile,
And thy sweet spells from sleep all living things
        beguile.

Delightful hour ! the first, the best,
    The brightest in glad Summer's train,
When man, refreshed by peaceful rest,
    Blithely resumes his toil again ;
Hope's angel-smiles through all thy beauties shine,
And all her charms, sweet morning hour, are thine.

NIGHT.

Oh, loveliest hour of all that bless
Earth with their passing loveliness,
Calm night! when sinks in deep repose,
Each care, each toil, that daylight knows :
To me, than Summer's noonday glare,
More dear thou art, more sweetly fair.

Canst thou be all of earth, when oft
Upon the heart thine influence soft
Falls, as from Heaven a healing shower,
So strangely deep its soothing power?
And must thy beauty pass away,
Thy softness yield to lasting day?

Yes! night, thy reign must soon be o'er;
Thy calm shall soothe the heart no more;
Thy task fulfilled, thy mission done,
When earth its latest course has run;
No need for night, no need for rest,
When Heaven's own glory fills the breast.

THE SIEGE.

There was of old a maiden citadel,
   And for it two great powers contested long;
Humility besieged—so legends tell—
   But Pride still held the inner fortress strong:
Humility had gained the outer wall,
And hung his banners there, but that was all.

But after a long time, a stranger came
   To the besieger's camp, and promised aid.
His name was Love, a strategist of fame,
   And many were the conquests he had made;
He travelled in a low and simple guise,
And Pride might well such power as his despise.

Love went to work with mining tools, and sought
   A passage through the living rock below;
Day after day, and hour by hour, he wrought
   With hopeful progress, still, albeit slow:
At length he found a low, unguarded cave,
That to the inner fortress entrance gave.

Then he and that great chief, Humility,
   Together entered by the secret way;

And Pride, who dreamed not of defeat so nigh,
    Fled from his high command in sore dismay;
So peace was made within; but from that hour
Humility and Love held equal power.

IMOGEN.

" Ere I could tell him
How I would think on him at certain hours
Such thoughts, and such."
—CYMBELINE.

FALL gently, gently, shades of night !
  Rise up, sweet moon, o'er hill and dale,
And shed from yonder tree-crowned height
  Your silver radiance, pure and pale.

Blow on, soft breeze, and bear away
  The idle words that pain my ear ;
The jarring voices of the day,
  A little while, I need not hear.

Now all is still—the fresh, calm air
  Brings me the fragrant souls of flowers ;
Ah ! would, my love, that it could bear,
  At least, a messenger from ours.

Vain fancy ! yet I need but sleep
  And straight behold thee in my dream,
Pictured on mem'ry's mirror deep,
  Clear as the heavens on Severn's stream.

For when cold Reason yields her reign,
  And outward sense lies dead and still,
Love opes the portals of the brain,
  And ushers in the guest he will.

Good night, dear love, thou too mayst hail
  The breathing of these zephyrs light ;
Oh, fly to greet him, gentle gale,
  And whisper low, Good night—good night !

WOMEN'S RIGHTS.

You cannot rob us of the rights we cherish,
   Nor turn our thoughts away
From the bright picture of a " Woman's Mission "
   Our hearts pourtray.

We claim to dwell, in quiet and seclusion,
   Beneath the household roof,—
From the great world's harsh strife, and jarring voices,
   To stand aloof ;—

Not in a dreamy and inane abstraction
   To sleep our life away,
But, gathering up the brightness of home sunshine,
   To deck our way.

As fragrant plants by country hedgerows growing,
   That treasure up the rain,
And yield in odours, ere the day's declining,
   The gift again ;

So let us, unobtrusive and unnoticed,
   But happy none the less,
Be privileged to fill the air around us
   With happiness ;

To live, unknown beyond the cherished circle
 Which we can bless and aid ;
To die, and not a heart that does not love us
 Know where we're laid.

EVENING.

HUSHED is the thunder,
  The storm has passed by.
Floats not a rain-cloud
  Across the clear sky ;
In the west lingers
  The glory of day,
Gleams on the mountains
  Its last golden ray.

In the dark forest
  The breeze is at rest,
Not a wave ruffles
  The lake's silver breast ;
Gently the flowers
  Have sunk to repose,
Softly among them
  The rivulet flows.

One fair star beaming
  In radiance above,
Sheds o'er their slumbers
  The pure light of love ;

Calm, serene, tender,
    The aspect she wears,
Her smile celestial,
    Shining through tears.

All the wide landscape
    Lies silent and still
No sound in the valley,
    No voice on the hill;
Slowly the bright tints
    Fade from the sky;
Risen in splendour
    The moon floats on high.

Night in her beauty
    Descends on the land;
Dewdrops are scattered
    Like pearls from her hand;
O'er bird, tree, and flower,
    Her pure gifts she throws;
To man, worn and weary,
    She giveth repose.

THE OLD WIFE.

YES, she is old—she must be old,
   For I remember long ago
Her tresses gleamed like living gold,
   That now are white as drifted snow,
And the pure oval of her face,
   The fair round cheek and sunny brow,
The pliant form's unrivalled grace
   Have lost their early freshness now.

Old—yet believe it as you will,
   The tender beauty fair and bright,
That stirs me in remembrance now
   As when I first beheld its light,
Was not, nor could be, half so dear,
   As are the looks I meet to-day,
Where Time has given with every year
   More charms than e'er he stole away.

For in her face I love to read
   The records of her faithful love,
My solace in each hour of need,
   My anchor that no storm could move :

For me each day of care she bore,
    For me and mine the tears she shed ;
Rememb'ring all, I can but pour
    A thousand blessings on her head.

A BALLAD.

" Mother ! open the door,
    The wind blows chilly and bleak ;
Mother ! open the door,
    For I'm growing faint and weak."
Up she rose from the fire,
    Rose up from her lonely watch,
Quickly she went to the door,
    And quickly lifted the latch.

Out she looked on the night,
    The wind blew bitter and shrill,
But nothing there could she see,
    And the voice she had heard was still :
Back with a heavy sigh,
    She went to her fireside seat,
But the voice was there once more,
    And the sound of childish feet.

She leaned her over the bed,
    Her lips were parched and blue,
The eyes of the dying were open wide,
    And she saw that he heard it too.

His eyes were open wide
  With a ghastly look of dread,
And, when she had watched him a moment's space,
  She turned away from the dead !

She opened the door again,
  And looked out through the tempest wild,
And there she saw, at the forest side,
  The form of a little child.
With a cry of anguish and fear,
  She rushed to where it stood,
But its garments were gleaming farther on
  In the darkness of the wood.

Still, she followed it fast,
  And still, it flitted before,
Until she thought her weary limbs
  Would bear her on no more ;
Still, as the night wore on,
  She followed the flying shade,
Till she came to an old stone carvèd cross,
  And there knelt down and prayed.

There, with a breaking heart,
  She prayed to be cleansed within ;
That her mind might be freed from its deadly chain,
  And her soul be washed from sin.

She prayed till the light was faint
   In the east, when a slumber stole
Over her weary senses,
   Soothing her guilty soul.

The trees were dripping above her,
   The skies were stormy and wild,
But she saw naught in her slumber
   Save the form of a little child.
The child stood close beside her,
   And spoke in accents low,
Not like the tones of terror
   That haunted her, hours ago.

" Mother, here in the forest
   You left me to starve and die,
And here, where my bones are bleaching,
   Your lifeless corpse must lie ;
But now, the gates of Heaven
   May open to let you in,
For true and hearty repentance
   Has washed away your sin."

Up rose the sun in his glory
   And lighted the forest glade,
And shone on the old stone cross
   Where the woman's form was laid ;

The grass grew high around her
   Heavy with dew and rain,
But she lay wrapped in a slumber
   That never knew waking again.

A PEEP AT THE FAIRIES.

COME out, come out of the stifling rooms,
　Come out in the Summer air ;
The cool night winds blow over the fields,
The fragrant sweetbriar its perfume yields,
　And the skies are bright and fair.

And see, oh see, o'er the smooth mown grass
　The flickering lights that play ;
Are they the firefly's lamps that gleam ?
No ! by the brightness of every beam,
　The fairies keep holiday.

Now, for the roof of their festal hall,
　A sweetbriar spray is bent ;
And for curtains of tissue, silvery white,
Studded with wonderful pearls of light,
　A spider his web has lent.

Yonder, two elves with all their might
　Come dragging a mighty stone ;
A pure white pebble, smooth and fair—
Now they have placed it, with heed and care,
　'Tis surely meant for a throne !

E.

What will they do for a canopy?
   Ingenious elves are they—
See! they have hung a roseleaf sweet
Floating over the royal seat,
   Under the sweetbriar spray.

A large, smooth leaf from a laurel bough
   Some friendly wind has rent,
This shall their festal table be
Loaded with spoils of flower and bee,
   Laid 'neath the cobweb tent.

Hark! I hear from the thicket side
   The sound of a fairy horn,
Soft as the dewdrops on the grass,
The trickling rills of music pass,
   On flitting breezes borne.

And now they come, in martial state
   Surrounding their tiny Queen;
Gentles and Dames, a courtly train—
And, marching in time to the minstrel strain,
   Come archers in garb of green.

All lit by the fairy torchlight's gleam
   They wind o'er the dewy sod:

And the green blades spring from the pressure light,
And the uncrushed daisies glimmer white,
   Where an instant past they trod.

No more must we gaze,—some hurtful spell
   Still follows the curious eye ;
And evil befalls the luckless wight,
Who dares in the starry Summer night
   Intrude on their revelry.

SONG.

Not when the Summer days
    Glide softly by;
Not when the lark's sweet lays
    Float from the sky;
Not when bird, flower, and bee
Fill earth with melody,
Let one sad thought of me
    Waken thy sigh.

And when the Winter fire
    Sheds its clear light;
Just ere the year expire
    That rose so bright;
When laughter's silver sound,
And the glad song goes round,
Be no dark memory found
    Haunting the night.

But when the silent hour
    Of man's deep rest
Bids memory's sleepless power
    Reign in thy breast,

Then, let the thought of me
Float through the air to thee,
And in thy visions be
    A welcome guest.

ITALY—1870.

PHŒNIX of Nations! from the smould'ring heap
  Of ashes, whence thou spread'st thy radiant wing,
  How have we watched and joyed to see thee spring
In vigorous life, as one refreshed by sleep!
Now, smiles illume the eyes, that wont to weep,
  And blessings, from afar, are o'er thee shed,
  While Freedom's children greet thy crownèd head.
We, from her island seat, amid the deep,
We, who have sorrowed for thy hour of pain,
  Now bid thee, on thy brightening way, "God
    speed!"
May He, whose Spirit can alone make free,
Whose word hath called thee into life again,
Preserve thee evermore in every need,
  And twine the olive wreath of peace for thee.

"*ABIDE WITH US.*"

"ABIDE with us—the hours of day are waning,
And gloomy skies proclaim th' approach of night ;
Leave us not yet, but, with us still abiding,
Cheer us until the morning's welcome light."

"Abide with us—before Thy gentle teaching
The clouds of grief that wrapped our spirits fly,
And to our inmost souls thine influence reaching
Lays all our unbelief and terror by."

"Abide with us—oh! when our hearts were failing,
How did Thy words revive our dying faith,
The hidden prophecies of old unveiling,
Showing the mysteries of Messiah's death."

"Abide with us "—so prayed they, though unknowing
Him who had cheered them with His words divine ;
So, Lord, with us abide, Thy peace bestowing,
Till every heart become Thy living shrine.

THE DAY DAWN.

As when the heavy shades of night
   Begin to yield before the dawn,
And first a grey and misty light
   Creeps slowly over grove and lawn,
Until above the purpled hills
   Long level rays their glory pour,
And light the whole wide circle fills,
   And life, where all seemed dead before.

So slowly bright'ning o'er the soul
   Until the shadows flee away,
While night's dark clouds asunder roll
   And fade amid the perfect day,
Dost Thou, O Sun and Light Divine,
   In growing splendour clearly rise,
And bid the heavenly landscape shine
   Refulgent on our wondering eyes.

EVER WITH THEE.

No more in darkness, trials, and temptations,
No more a waif on trouble's billowy sea,
How sweet will be the day of our abiding
                 Ever with Thee !

Bright after darkness shines the Summer morning,
Bright is the sunshine when the tempests flee,
But brighter far the home where dwell Thy chosen
                 Ever with Thee.

Dear are the hours when those we love are near us,
Dear, but how transient must their sweetness be !
That one glad day will know no sadder morrow
                 Ever with Thee.

Love will be there—methinks all other glories
Nothing to those enraptured souls will be,
Filled with the transport of that one assurance,
                 " Ever with Thee."

But long may be the way that we must travel,
And many a dark'ning storm we yet may see,
Dread sorrows may o'erwhelm us ere we're sheltered
                 Ever with Thee.

Not so : Thy hand, extended through the darkness,
Leadeth us on the way we cannot see ;
And, clasping that, e'en here we walk in safety
      Ever with Thee.

"*TOUCHED WITH THE FEELING OF OUR INFIRMITIES.*"

THOU giv'st the morning's early dew,
　　The day's awakening light,
The noontide beam, the cool of eve,
　　The stillness of the night;
Thou daily dost our strength renew,
　　And, when our labours close,
Thou watchest by the silent couch
　　And guardest our repose.

Is there a thought within our brain,
　　A fancy unexpressed,
That will not clothe itself in words
　　To mortal ears addressed?
Yet Thou hast seen it from its rise,
　　And read'st, whate'er it be,
And even the visions of our sleep
　　Are known, O Lord, to Thee!

Have we a grief in silence borne
　　No human eye can see,
Blooms there a joy within our hearts
　　We breathe not e'en to Thee?

Thou seest, Thou feel'st, and giv'st us back,
    Alike in joy or woe,
A thrill of finer sympathy
    Than earth can e'er bestow.

Oh ! this, beyond the richest store
    Of outward gifts divine,
This proves to many a grateful soul
    That boundless love of Thine ;
A love that guards through childhood's years,
    That cheers Life's devious way,
And bears from Death's victorious dart
    The venomed sting away.

THE LAMB IS THE LIGHT THEREOF.

THE fairest light that ever shone
    In Summer skies,
The purest rays that ever flashed
    On mortal eyes,
Shall be but as the dead of night
To that eternal, glorious light
    That shall be given
To those who, for a little space,
Have bravely run the Christian race
    And entered Heav'n.

Sometimes a gleam of that pure light
    Is found below
In humble hearts that on their way
    With patience go.
It makes those hearts with rapture bound :
And, though the scene be dark around,
    It cheers them on,
Augments and brightens day by day,
And still emits a purer ray,
    Till life is done.

That spotless sun, which ever lights
        Heaven's peaceful clime,
Which no mutation knows, nor shade
        Of night or time,
Is but the reflex of His love
Who, slain for us, now reigns above,
        Our Saviour-God :
And, while on high His glory's shed,
He guides the pilgrim feet that tread
        Where once He trod.

THE SIXTEENTH PSALM.

PRESERVE me, Lord, for in Thy strength
  My trust shall ever be ;
My soul, with childlike faith and hope,
  Shall still repose on Thee.

Thy saints are dear unto my heart,
  And those that love Thy way ;
But from the dangerous paths of sin
  I'll turn my eyes away.

Thou, Lord, Thyself, shalt be my lot,
  And, while Thy love is mine,
I'm owner of a fair domain,
  A heritage divine.

For this my heart shall still rejoice,
  For this my songs shall rise,
Nor Death shall chill the certain hope
  That points to yonder skies.

Thy power can break his icy chains,
  Can set his prisoners free,
And raise the souls that Thou hast made
  To dwell in Heaven with Thee.

NIGHT MUSINGS.

Now Night has closed around us,
   And Sleep her wings has spread
O'er many a silent pillow,
   O'er many a weary head,
And thousand changeful visions
   Through Fancy's mazes stray,
Where mingle forms of Faëry
   With those of yesterday.

No dreams can weave their network
   Around my brain to-night,
No fancied forms are treading
   That path of silver light ;
The moon of Thy ordaining,
   The stars that own Thy word,
Look through my window, telling
   The goodness of the Lord.

Nor they alone are speaking
   Their mighty Maker's praise,
While each eventful moment
   Thy fixed decree obeys ;

The breathing of the sleepers,
The stillness of the hour,
The calm that reigns about us,
Attest Thy Love and Power.

GENIUS.

Envy not, thought of mine, those whose rich dower
Is genius, Heaven's most dazzling gift to men ;
Admire, but envy not ; for oh ! to them,
Great is the peril wedded to the power.
Blest, trebly blest, if in each dangerous hour
  Religion guides them with her ray divine ;
    Then, on their kind, like Spring's sweet days they
        shine
With vivifying gifts of sun and shower ;
But awful is the might, and dread the doom,
  Of genius unennobled and unblest,
    Whose gleam is but the lightning's baleful ray,
Flashing with fatal splendour through the gloom ,
Death-fraught and dying : let me rather rest
  Where on my sheltered path may beam the day.

RETROSPECTION.

'Tis not well to forget—it is good to recall,
  As we bask in the sunshine, the storms that have
    been,
When the joy of the present shines bright over all.
  To remember a moment the darkness we've seen;
For there was not a day when some light did not
    break
  Like an angel from Heaven, thro' the tempest's dark
    shroud,
And Hope with fresh smiles from her slumber awake,
  As the fair bow of promise shone bright on the
    cloud.

'Tis not well to forget,—in the night of the soul
  'Tis well that our visions should be of the past :
Thus assured that the shadows asunder will roll,
  And leave us a morning as bright as the last :
For the Hand that has guided is guiding us still ;
  By the way that He led us He leadeth us yet,
And sorrow's dark terrors, or pleasure's keen thrill,
  May whisper alike, "'Tis not well to forget."

SONG OF THE LEAF.

LEAF, young and fair,
Tossed on the Summer air—
   Is it not sweet to thee
Part of so bright a world to be?
"Yes, it is sweet to the morning sun,
   Offering my dewdrops one by one—
Sweeter still when the shadows fall,
And stars are glimmering over all."

   Yet thou must fall ;
Soon at chill Autumn's call,
   Storms from the icy north
Armed 'gainst thy happy life, come forth.
"Yes, I must fall when Summer is past,
   Must far from the storm-swept bough be cast,
Be crushed and soiled by some passing tread,
Only a leaf, all brown and dead!"

   Why so elate,
Looking to such a fate?
   Dost thou not fear to die
Under the frowns of Winter's sky?

" Yes, I should tremble with fear and pain,
 Knew I not this, ' I shall live again,'
 Fresh life shall spring from the short decay,
 Therefore I dance in the Summer day."

GUIDANCE.

As evening fell, the cloud abode
 Above a bleak and sterile plain ;
And quickly tents were spread abroad.
 The dwellings of a wandering train.

But why—where neither silvery stream.
 To wet their parching lips, was near.
Nor grass their cattle to sustain—
 Why did the people linger here?

" At the commandment of the Lord,"
 Around the symbol of His care,
They stayed obedient to His word,
 Enough for them that He was there.

And mid them through the silent night
 Shone clear and bright His beacon flame,
Nor paled its glorious, awful light,
 Until the sun of morning came.

Where'er they saw, by night or day,
 The cloud, the fire, they followed still.
Nor erred upon their pathless way,
 Guided by one unerring will.

Thou who didst lead the tribes of old
   Through deserts drear by paths unknown,
And daily stores of love unfold,
   To succour and to shield Thine own ;

Oh ! through the void of sorrow's night,
   When all perplexed and lost we stray,
Vouchsafe to us Thy guiding light,
   At once to point and cheer the way.

LINES TO A FRIEND.

March, 18*th*.

I WOULD have had you see to-day, my friend,
How beauteously our Canada can vie
With our still dearer England, in the charm
Of sky and lake and river.   Here no fields,
Here, in this western wilderness afar,
With soft rich verdure, rest the grateful eye,
But, on a day like this, we think no more
Of what *would* please us, but of what *does* please.

The sky was cloudless ; of that loveliest blue,
Not dark, but like the bright forget-me-not,
That jewel of the hedgerows—with a clear,
Soft, pure transparence, the best gift of Spring.
And then our river ! oft, I love to watch
Its dancing, rippling waters, and to-day
They had an added dower of loveliness.
All over its bright surface, deeply blue,
Glittered and sparkled with a thousand rays,
Gems, coronals, and chains of broken ice.
I could have dreamt the genii of the lamp
Had heaped the waters with the costly freight

Of jewels, for Aladdin's matchless pile.
Long stood I on the shore, and could not tear
My feasted eyes from such a lovely scene,
Till the clear waters 'gan be tinged with gold,
And, slowly, slowly, westward sank the sun.

Then what a glory crested every wave!
And every gem, that shone and gleamed before,
Shot forth a million sparks of coloured flame,
Crimson and green and blue.   Beyond, the pines,
Far off, against th' horizon, let the light
Break through them in long, level rays, and showed
Like a dark network on the glowing sky.
High in the heavens some clouds—I know not whence
They came, for just before there was not one—
Majestically floated, robed in hues
Of matchless beauty.   Those which highest lay
Were tinted with that pure and delicate green
You've seen on pearl-like sea shells, with an edge
Of softly shaded rose.   A lower tier,
In rich, resplendent gold and purple, shone;
And all above, around, below, the hue
Of the clear ether gradually changed
From loveliest azure to the deepest tints
Of glowing crimson.

                                        Ah! but what avail
My feeble words to tell what never yet
The highest genius called to perfect life
Upon his canvas?   Yet 'tis not in vain
That I have tried to reproduce for thee
The scene I loved to look on— not in vain.
For writing thus, I, in my thought, have heard
Again the voice that spoke from stream and sky
Silently eloquent, and said, " Behold
The glory of God's footstool !   What must be
The brightness of His throne ?   To Him, then, raise
Thy wonder and thy worship evermore."

THE BALLAD SINGER.

It was a street, where still, from morn till eve,
Flowed on the living tide with ceaseless swell ;
A thousand different faces passed it by,
A thousand different footsteps trod its stones,
But, ever as they came, they seemed to bear,
On wrinkled brows and in their restless eyes,
The seal that stamps the votaries of wealth.
    So passed they daily—it had been as strange
To see, amid that dry and trodden way,
A rose-tree in luxuriant wealth of bloom,
As there to meet a face untouched by care.
One day, the busiest passers caught a sound
Unwonted there—" What is it ? "   " Oh ! pass on.
'Tis but a ballad singer."   Yet that voice,
Clearly harmonious, heard above the din,
As though those silver notes were all too pure
To mix with baser sounds, had some strange charm,
And stayed some hasty steps—'twas thus she sang :

        I am blind, and the light is gone,
            For ever is gone from me,
        I dwell in the city alone,
        I wander its pathways of stone,

Yet ever I seem to see
A beautiful home, where the sun shines bright,
All rich in the beauty of verdure and light.

There's a tree by the garden gate,
    Where the birds sing all day long,
And a seat, where they often wait
When the tranquil eve grows late
    For the nightingale's lovelier song;
And beyond, a meadow slopes gently away,
Where they hear the laugh of the children at play.

There peeps from the windows bright
    A spirit of heartfelt peace,
And Winter and Summer, and day and night,
It blesses the household with calm delight,
    And pleasures that never cease ;
'Tis the pure home love that hallows the spot,
And sheds its light o'er that peaceful cot.

JOAN OF ARC.

PART I.

A WILD hillside beneath the winds of March—
With scattered sheep upon the tufted grass,
And here and there a tree, grotesque and lone,
Strong limbed, but stunted, like a sturdy dwarf
Misshapen, leafless.   Overhead the clouds
Travelled with varying motion from the east ;
Hurried, yet sullen ; lagging on the breeze.

Up the rough path, that wound among the furze,
Slowly, with serious eyes that looked before
(Her soul not seeing what their vision saw),
With steps that knew the path too well to stray,
Moving, as habit, not as thought, ordained,
Came, through the chilly eve, a girl's slight form ;
It was not till she gained the rounded brow,
Where east and north and south the hill sloped down
And showed the winding valley far below,
She turned and looked.   Down there beneath her feet,
And sheltered by the huge arms of the hills
(Like a small nest amid the sturdy boughs
Whose well-tried strength defies the wildest storm),
The pleasant village, with its humble spire,

Lay calm and tranquil; and the little streams,
Fed from the sunless caverns of the rocks,
Joining their slender threads of silver, ran
Through meadows, where a strip of level ground
Was bright with springing grass. A lovely scene
To stranger eyes, to hers 'twas more, 'twas home!
There, as she stood and looked, a sudden gust
Came right across the valley, bitter cold,—
She drew her mantle closer round her breast
And faced it boldly, while a vivid glow
Began to kindle in her soft, dark eye,
Gleamed like a beacon through a Summer night,
Lighting her pallid cheek and thoughtful brow,
Till, with a sigh of smothered passion, broke,
From quivering lips—"Would I could die to save,
To save thee, O my country!---but I fear"—
So, with drooped eyes, she turned away and went
To seek her scattered flock and bring them home.

Clear from the village belfry rang the bell;
The gathered flocks, from mountain pastures led,
Were safely housed, and up the stony street
Came the small throng of evening worshippers.
Among them, with an old man by her side,
Came the pale shepherd girl, the dark-eyed Joan,
Of whom men said, she saw strange sights, and heard

Voices that others hear not.   On they passed.
Soon rose the music of the evening prayer
Artlessly sweet, and floated to the skies
With sprinkled incense, on the darkening air.

The prayers were ended.   Over each bowed head
The priest had poured his blessing ; all were gone
But Joan, who yet before St. Catherine's shrine
Was kneeling, lost in prayer.   Her fingers held
Her half told rosary, now all forgot,
Forgot the oft-said words—her eager thoughts
Shaped themselves into fervid life and knocked
At Heaven's high gate for entrance.   By and by.
Her cheeks aglow, her frame with ardour thrilled,
She saw a dawning light break from the crown
That bound the saint's fair brow, and down it
    stole,
Enveloping the figure in a haze
Of golden splendour, while the sweet face wore
A heavenly smile, and from the carvèd lips
A soft voice uttered, " Joan, be strong of heart,
Take courage to fulfil thy own deep wish,
For thine it is to save thy native land."

Faded the smile, while yet the gazer bent
Her tear-suffusèd eyes upon its beam—

Slowly the light died out, and naught was left
But her enraptured fancy echoing yet,
"Joan, it is thine to save thy native land."
Listening to this dear echo, long she knelt,
Till, through her dazzling dream, she faintly heard
A step upon the creaking belfry stair,
And the first note of curfew broke the spell.

Beneath the shadow of her father's roof
Joan passed and laid her down, but hours flew by
Ere sleep's soft pinions fanned her heated brain ;
And when, at length, she slept, sweet dreams again
Repeated the sweet vision of the eve—
But not for long her slumber or her bliss.

When after midnight scarce two hours were flown,
Wild through the silence rang a fearful cry,
Then, swiftly following, shrieks, and oaths, and screams,
The tramp of horses, and the trumpet's blast,
While women shrieked, " They come ! the spoilers
        come ! "
And fled with wailing babes out through the night.

Happy were they who saved in that dread hour
Their lives and those they loved, although they stood
With Joan and that small household on the hill,

And watched the wreathing flames extend their arms
Till every dwelling shared the fell embrace.
A fearful sight—the sky glowed overhead,
And tenfold darker seemed th' abyss of night
Around those blazing walls, those ruined homes.

Darkly, amid the glare, the old church tower
Showed the sad people that the house of God
Stood scathless 'mid the wreck, but, oh! the cry
With which they marked the first red flame that twined
About the carving of the sacred door,
And, quickly spreading, mounted to the roof.
Kneeling upon the turf, with streaming hair,
With eyes of horror, and tight-clasping hands,
Joan watched the burning rafters till they fell
And darkened the full glare of lurid light;
Then rose, and, turning from the village, flung
Her arms about a young tree standing near
And hid her face upon them, while her heart
Cried out in her, "O God, deliver France!"
And made an answer to herself, and said,
"He will deliver us—a time will come,
Is coming quickly, to avenge our wrongs."

PART II.

Now many days had passed since that dread time,
When sudden violence disturbed the night
To scatter death and ruin all around.
Back to their desolated homes again
The villagers had wandered from the hills
And desert places of their sudden flight.
Joan with her father came, and helped to raise
Some wretched shelter from the cold and storm,
Where they might light their household fires again.
   Darker and deeper since that awful hour,
Through days of misery when her heart was wrung
With sights and sounds of suffering, grew her thoughts.
Now ceaselessly she heard a voice that cried,
" Go forth, ordained of Heaven, to save thy land ! "
Strange visions visited her broken sleep,
And once St. Catherine stood beside her bed
Divinely beautiful, in robes of light,
With grave, unsmiling brightness in her eyes.
Thus spoke she—" Wherefore dost thou linger here ?
Thy country calls for thee, the promised maid,
Appointed by high Heaven to rescue France.
Rise, seek the King, for even now his mind
Is sore oppressed with evil.   Tell him all—
And bid him greet the future as his friend,

For thou shalt stand beside him when the crown
Circles his brow in peace. Yet, if he need
Proof of thy mission, bid him quickly send
To where my holy fane of Firebois lifts
Its hoary head, and in a coffer old,
Dusty with age, and half by rust consumed,
There they shall find an ancient sword blade, marked
With three rude crosses. Let them bring it thee,
For by that weapon, and our Lady's help,
Thou shalt recover France." So Joan awoke.
From thenceforth all her mind was set in her
To leave her village and her aged sire,
Travelling to seek the King : and weeks passed by
Slowly as years, until she found a time,
And, after many prayers and vigils kept,
Set forth upon her mission from her home.

PART III.

'Twas a high day in Rheims—the sunlit streets
Were flooded full with life, and up and down
Rang the gay clangour of the burnished arms.
Pennons and scarfs and feathers waved in air,
And all of regal, all of martial state,
That France could muster, glittered round her King :
For, now, the coronation oath was said,

And, now, the golden circlet, rich with gems,
With hallowing prayers was placed upon his head.
Forth from the crowd uprose a joyous cry,
" Long live King Charles the Seventh! " uprose and
    swelled,
Over the swaying multitude around.
    Bright through its space the vast cathedral gleamed
With arms, with beauty clothed in rich attire—
With priests in gorgeous vestments, mixed with men
In many a battle scarred—but near the King,
White robed above her glimmering suit of mail,
Holding a snowy banner in her hand,
And girded with her still victorious sword,
Stood the heroic maid, the prop of France.
Could this be she—the simple country girl,
Who watched her father's flock upon the hill,
Or knelt among the village worshippers?
Had not this splendour changed her? for she stood,
Honoured among the nobles of the land,
Deliverer of her country in its need.
No! in the mournful paleness of her brow,
The strange, sad beauty of her clear brown eyes,
And firm, sweet mouth, still looked there forth the
    soul,
Once wrung with anguish for her country's woes,
And now, far looking onward to her own.

When all the rites were done, she slowly turned,
Kneeling before the King, and humbly spoke—
" My liege, my work is done—when first I came
From my wild mountain home, and dared to stand,
I, a poor village girl, amid your Court,
And promise boldly (what is now performed)
That this glad day should come, and through my help,
I but obeyed a loftier will than mine,
Inspired of Heaven to serve my country's need ;
But now that need is past—my work is done—
Now let me go, back to my father's cot,
Back to my brother's dwelling—to my home ! "

" Nay," said the King, " not so, we need thee still :
Thou, who hast led our troops to victory,
Shalt lead them yet, we cannot part with thee ;
But meet it is, on such a day as this,
That we, such honour as a sovereign may,
So poor as we are, should bestow on thee—
Henceforth we make thee noble through all time ;
Thou, and thy brothers, and thy aged sire,
And every one descended of thy line—
And, when our budding fortunes shall permit,
Fit revenue to prop thy rank shall be
Added to honours. Wilt thou leave us now ?
Well, then, if state and wealth can move thee not,

Listen, O maiden ! to thy country's voice—
Still do the rude invaders tread her plains,
Still many a cruel deed of hideous war
Lays her fair dwellings waste.   Return not yet!
She cries to thee, and Heaven will aid thee still."
He ceased.   Before her sad and troubled eyes
What varying visions floated ! but at last
She said, " I will not go," and sealed her doom.

PART IV.

Another city, and another scene—
An ancient city, o'er whose painted roofs
And many towers, perchance, the heavens were dark
With angry clouds and storms—perchance, the sun
Smiled in his brightness—what was it to her?
She only knew it was her day to die !

Through the barred windows when the earliest dawn
Crept to her prison chamber, she was there
Kneeling before her little crucifix
Praying, until the murmured prayer was lost
In a wild rush of memory.   Back they came,
Her peaceful days of childhood—floated back
Her village home, the hillside, and the breeze.
And, strangely clear, the ringing of the bell.

Then, she was kneeling at St. Catherine's shrine,
Hearing again the silver tones that said,
" To thee is given to save thy native land."
And fancy bore her on from field to field,
From day to day of glory, till the last,
That highest hour of triumph, when she stood
Beside, while hoary prelates crowned the King.
　　Thence onward still, and still through victory,
But now no more she foremost—others came
And entered on her labours and her place.
And worse than all—the voices that had cheered—
The fearless faith in Heaven's high guidance—failed,
Doubts clustered round her, doubts of her own self
Tracking her footsteps darkly, till the night
Of blackest mis'ry when she knew herself
A prisoner, and deserted. " Woe to those,"
She cried aloud in bitterness, " who place
Their trust in princes !　Was there not a knight
In all the noble army of the King
Could lift his arm for me, who saved the crown?"
Then, weeping passionate tears, began again
Her broken prayers.　So wore the early hours,
Till, by and by, her cruel jailers came,
And yet more cruel priests, who, with Christ's name
Upon their impious lips, could torture her,
That wretched woman, in her agony ;

For now, no more sustained by lofty hopes,
Her spirit turned in anguish on itself,
Making wild conflict in her troubled breast,
Till at the last, when they had wrought their will,
And she, to save herself, with trembling hand
Had signed the dread confession of her crime,
Branding her memory with the double guilt
Of witchcraft, and denial of her faith,
They left her for awhile, and in that hour
Peace came upon her soul, and she was calm,
Looking for death as for a welcome guest.

At length they led her forth.   Amid a crowd
Of thousands, as in other days, she moved :
Then, all was acclamation where she came ;
Now, a dread silence reigned.   The stake was reared
Amidst the open square, that all might see ;
And many another goodly sight was there :
Princes and priests, rich-robed and gay with gems,
Knights in bright armour, and no lack of men,
Such as seemed human, come to look on her.
They bound her fast—she, scarce alive to thought,
Seeing them heap the faggots round her form,
Seeing the cruel faces of the throng,
No pity anywhere—grew cold as ice,
And shivered while she looked, not knowing why ;

So, in a trance of horror wrapped, she stood,
They deeming that she listened, while a monk
Told all her grievous sins aloud, and showed
In the great audience of the people there
Her guilt and her confession. When he ceased,
The fire was brought, and soon the kindled pile,
Flaming around her, with rude shock called back
Each power of suffering. Then she wildly shrieked,
And, holding up her cherished crucifix,
Called upon Him whose sacred form it bore,
Her last, sole refuge, for His pity then.
So the flame swept above her guiltless head,
And, with His name upon her lips, she died.

BOSCOBEL.

HALF hidden in the circle of thy woods
Thou standest yet, unchanged and beautiful,
Thrice-honoured relic of a famous time !
On history's page thou livest, but far more
In hearts that having loved thee, love thee still,
And keep thy smile in memory.   On thy sward
The every varying shadows dance and play,
And on thy grassy mound the daisies spring
New yearly, yet the same—the very flowers
Are blooming in thy quaint parterres that bloomed
Two hundred years ago.
           I scarce can think
It was not yesterday the wanderer came—
That homeless wanderer—that uncrowned King—
Who, in his perilous and desperate plight,
Swayed England's loyal hearts with deeper power
Than when he held the sceptre—that he came
Seeking thy shades for safety.   Then, all day,
The ceaseless Summer rain that drenched thy boughs
Seemed weeping for the kingdom's downfall—he,
Meanwhile, must make his royal couch and throne
Beneath thy dripping leaves.   Weary, oppressed,
Heart-sick, and sad, by disappointment chilled

More than by wet or hunger, he must watch
The long hours through, nor dare to venture forth,
Lest death be lingering near.
                              Yet was he not
Deserted—there were noble hearts and true
Watching and labouring for their outcast King.
Alas! that he to whom such faith was given
Proved so unworthy! that the promise bright
He gave in danger and distress should be
Like the white hoar frost on the morning grass,
And, when the sun of happier fortune rose,
Vanish in air.   But that is naught to thee;
Thou, in thy leafy covert art a shrine
Sacred to noblest virtues.   Be thou still,
Time-honoured spot, as sweet and fair as now;
No sacrilegious hand be ever raised
To mar with modern change thine ancient grace,
But be thou still, in tranquil beauty calm,
An ark of quiet 'mid life's changing scene;
And still, to generations yet unborn,
Repeat, in music, thy romantic tale.
Such scenes as thine, on England's verdant plains,
Make up her greatest charm, and dower her with
Matchless associations—for in her,
And in her hallowed shrines of bygone days,
We need not say, " Alas! for liberty !"

But liberty still lives, and, while we bless
With reverent love the good men of the past,
We proudly add, " Their spirit fires their sons,
And England's virtues, like her sturdy oaks,
Unhurt by age or storm, perennial spring."

IANTHE.

"IANTHE, golden haired!
Bright Hebe, in the glory and the bloom
Of her immortal youth, was not more fair
Than thou, O loveliest! when the slender boughs
Bent o'er thee, with their light leaves to caress
Thy long bright tresses—when upon the hill
Thy song resounded, and the joyous birds
Stopped their sweet warblings, but to learn of thee.
The river, when thy white and glancing feet
Pressed its smooth pebbles, played around thy form
In brighter eddies, with a murmuring song,
Such as young mothers sing above their babes.
But now, we miss thee on the mountain slopes,
And in the hamlets, and beside the stream ;
Fairest and best beloved, return, return !"
So sang they in the valleys where they dwelt,
The white-browed daughters of that sunny isle—
And echo sadly gave the burden back—
Echo alone—and sighed, "Return, return ! "
But never more, beside the forest shade,
Or rocky beach, at evening's calmest hour,
They hailed thy form, Ianthe, brightest maid,
Or caught the silvery murmurs of thy song.

'Twas in a year long past, when Summer days
Had waned in cloudless glory to the prime
Of vintage and luxuriant harvest fields,
When darkly o'er the heavens swept up the clouds,
Hiding the sunlight, and, for many days
Shrouding the isle in darkness.   All around
The great sea-billows raised their foam-white crests
And dashed them on the beach with angry roar,
While the tall trees upon the swelling hills
Bent with strange gusts and howling savage winds.
The islesmen in wild terror sought the grove
Where holiest rites were done, and brought with them
Their costliest sacrifice and choicest gifts
To win the gods to mercy.   All day long
The priest stood by the altar offering up
(It seemed so) vain prayers, vainer sacrifice,
Till suddenly at eve, on the fourth day,
There fell a blackness o'er the worshippers,
Darker than dark, and held them chained with awe ;
Then through the cloud a voice, but what it said
None, not those nearest to the altar, heard
Save the priest only, and he answered low,
With deep obeisance.   Then the horror passed,
And light, such as there was before, returned.

From close beside the altar spoke the priest :

" Friends, seek your homes to-night ; be sure of this,
The anger of the gods is not for naught,
Yet they are merciful.—Even now, behold,
The sky grows clearer. At to-morrow's dawn
Assemble here once more,—then will I tell
Heaven's high behest, and see that ye obey."
Away into the valleys, sore amazed,
Passed the long train of people, and the night
Sank down in calm and stillness, save that yet
The angry roaring waters rose and fell,
Boiling and surging round the beaten shore.

Morn came in glory, while the piled-up clouds
In the far west yet spoke of danger near,
Forbidding fear to slumber—and with morn
Came to the temple all the anxious throng,
Came, with his stately step and flowing robe,
The venerable priest. Amid a hush
So deep they heard the stirring of the leaves,
He spoke to those around : " Friends, countrymen !
Consider what is dearest, what is best,
Of all our fair isle's treasures. Ask your hearts,
What holds the largest portion of their love ?
And seek ye thus a stainless sacrifice—
For such the gods demand. Well! know we all
We have too much forgotten in our wealth

The ever-gracious givers, and have held
Our wives, our children, and whatever else
We call our own, too much as only ours ;
Wherefore the gods are angry, and command,
Ere night return, we cast from yonder rock
Into those fiercest waves a gift of price
No less than is our eyes' most treasured light,
Our hopes' best stay, our ages' comforter.
Thus only, losing one, the best of all,
Can other lives of us and ours be saved,
Devoted else and doomed, with this our isle."

He ceased, and silence reigned, while glance met
    glance
In speechless questioning, and mothers strained
Their infants to their breasts, and fathers turned
To look into their fair young daughters' eyes,
In trembling apprehension what would be
Next moment; but next moment every eye
Was turned on one who stood there pale and calm,
Ianthe, daughter of the aged priest,
The fairest of the daughters of the isle.
Then passed a sudden shudder through the crowd ;
" Not thee, not thee, Ianthe!" from each heart
Burst with a sudden anguish, but she stilled
With one mute gesture all the throng, and spoke :

"O father! friends beloved! if any be
Most fit to die in such a cause, 'tis I!
Thou knowest, father, I have ever led
A simple, innocent life, nor once have failed
To bring my daily offering to the gods,
With prayers and due observance, from a child;
Nor need I, friends, with gratitude repeat
How ye have ever blessed my glad, short life
With wealth of many hearts. I know full well
Ye will remember me with gentle thoughts,
And, best, will cheer my father's lonely age
For his Ianthe's sake." She paused, and then
Turned to her sire and knelt, and prayed him bless
His child's resolve. He, who had meanwhile stood
Rigid as marble statue, and as pale,
Forced back with effort stern the agony
That gathered at his heart. He laid his hand
Untrembling on the locks of clustered gold
That hid his child's sweet face, and said, "'Tis well:
Well, dear Ianthe, hast thou said—and now
Thy father gives thee, gladly, from his arms,
As thou hast given thyself."

Then there arose
A sound of bitter weeping, and a wail
Of hopeless sorrow from the morn till noon,

H

And then a speechless awe.   The eve drew on,
And sunset, when the dark and troubled sea
Must swallow up the jewel of the isle.

At last the hour was come.   Upon the rock,
White robed and crowned with flowers, Ianthe stood :
Pale, with a glowing lustre in her eyes
Undimmed by fear or weeping.   By her side,
Her father, wholly calm, except that still
His longing, loving gaze would follow her,
And tell the sickening anguish of his soul ;
But yet he faltered not, and, as the sun
Went slowly downward to the glittering sea,
Glittering at rest far distant, slowly dropped
His eyes one moment on the billows near,
Then bade the maidens clustered round commence
Their dedicating hymn.   The strain arose
Softly and tremulous, then sank again,
And rose once more, and would have quickly ceased
In tears and bursting sobs, but that one voice
Rose clear, and full, and sweet, and led them on ;
Thine, bright Ianthe !   Then the prayer was said,
And, 'mid an instant's pause of breathless pain,
She sprang, as springs the sea-bird, from the height,
And the dark waters hid her evermore.

THE EVENING WALK.

HERE let us rest awhile ;—this moss-grown trunk
Makes a luxurious seat, a throne, if e'er
Thrones are so free from care as we may be
In this our rustic palace ; high o'erhead
The arching boughs, that hold our roof of leaves,
Mock man's laborious tracery, and show
A mightier Architect ; no windows throw,
Though stained with loveliest hues, a light so pure,
So cool, so chaste, as, through the fluttering screen,
Steals down upon the flowers, and lends them grace ;
Down in yon hollow, hidden by the fern,
The noisy brook goes rushing on its way ;
The bee, unwearied by his day of toil,
Comes home rejoicing, with his fragrant load ;
The woodpecker sends echoes through the wood,
And timid squirrels, with their shining eyes,
Peep at us from among the withered leaves :
The bolder chipmonk sits upon a bough
And eyes us steadily—his small, shrill bark
Startling the birds upon their lofty perch.
Look at these flowers ;—our English flowers are fair,
And their familiar faces stir our hearts ;
But these are different ;—see, this one has leaves

H 2

Like the white water-lily, fragile, pure,
And shattered by a touch ;—a crimson stain
Is on each petal, as some wounded heart
Had shed its life-blood o'er the snowy cup,
And dyed it thus for ever.   Here is one
Alike in shape, but of a purple hue ;
And this might be a lily of the vale
Grown to gigantic size—the shining leaves
Have lost in width what they have gained in height,
But the flowers keep their semblance.   I have seen
This plant before—last year we found the roots,
But it was later, and the bloom was gone ;
Where the bells had been, scarlet berries hung,
Warm, glowing, in the shadows of the wood.

Here, are some yellow violets—not like those
We used to love ; these have no sweet perfume,
And their pale hue looks strange, unnatural ;
And here, are white and blue, but all alike
Strange to our eyes, and speechless to our hearts.
I like this lilac-tinted flower that creeps
Close to the ground—Titania might have wreathed
Its tiny blossoms in her hair ; and sweet,
Though faint, the odour that betrays its nook,
The only scented wild-flower we have found.
Here are more fairy blossoms, white as snow,

Gleaming like stars, that, tempted by the flowers,
Wandering from yon blue heaven above us spread,
Were caught among the leaves.—How exquisite
The form and veining of each silvery gem !

How softly fades the twilight !   But the night,
Though lovely, must not find us lingering here.
The moon will gild the tree-tops, and the stars
Shine on the dewy flowers, and on our seat,
While we turn homeward with our gathered wealth.
Our gleaming wealth of jewels richly wrought,
Gems eloquent to speak the Graver's praise.

IN THE CANADIAN WOODS.

PART I.

Nymphs of each woodland scene who wont to hold
Your Summer rambles through the forest old,
Ye lovely beings, ever young and fair,
With starry eyes and blossom-circled hair,
Do the long snows that Winter scatters round,
Veiling the red of Autumn's battle-ground,
Or the chill horrors that his storm-breath pours,
Affright your gentle presence from our shores?
Or is it that, remote from those fair climes
Where poets shrined your names in deathless rhymes,
This western world of ours ye ne'er have trod,
Slept in its shades, or frolicked on its sod?
Fain would I bid, by talisman or spell,
Your footsteps haunt the scenes I love so well,
Fain would I catch, in green and shadowy glade,
Your flitting forms, light glancing through the shade ;
But, howsoe'er it be, ye dwell not here,
Or close concealed, to mortals ne'er appear.
No infant hero, nourished by your care,
The victor-laurels of these realms shall wear ;
Nor statesman, through your inspiration great
Frame wiser laws to guide the rising state.

Yet have I seen, when Summer days were bright,
Or Summer heavens o'erhung the dewy night,
So rich a veil of loveliness outspread
O'er field and forest, vale and mountain-head,
As might have decked for your ethereal race
Their fittest home, their loveliest dwelling-place.

Bright are the memories (like the starry gleams
Shining athwart some forest of our dreams)
That light for us, unalterably sweet,
The glades which once we pressed with idle feet.
There Summer smiled in prodigal array,
And tireless birds beguiled the hours away ;
There the hot noon crept o'er us with a sigh,
Eve lingered long in sweet tranquillity,
And morning gave so rich a dower of dew
Some drops still gleamed when night fresh largess
    threw.
There with soft whispering played each gentle wind,
And the green branches kissed their playmates kind,
While one who sat the quivering boughs beneath
Might catch these murmurs from the wanderers'
    breath :

      Whisper, whisper, low and near,
      Whisper, lest yon flowers should hear—

From the distant billowy sea,
From the golden-blossomed lea,
To your soft and sweet caress,
To your smile and to your kiss,
Gentle leaves, we come, we come,
Bid us welcome to your home !

So the winds whispered to the trembling leaves
Smiling and sporting on the forest caves,
But the gay rovers fled ere day was o'er,
And their sad playmates sighed, "They come no
    more !"

Oh, verdant shade ! untrodden and apart,
Such spells as thine reign longest o'er the heart ;
It must be that some storms o'erspread thy sky,
It must be that thy blooming flowerets die,
But as I see thee in the flush of June,
Kissed by the sun, or sleeping 'neath the moon,
Thou art a spot where shadowy dryad well,
Or wandering faun, might unmolested dwell.

PART II.

One year when Autumn's hand did first unfold
Her glowing stores of crimson, russet, gold,

And hung them on the trees where Summer's reign,
But now disputed, seemed not yet to wane,
We sought that narrow chasm's rocky side,
Where Montmorenci pours its headlong tide—
Those clear, brown waters from their forest home
Rush down begemmed with floating wreaths of foam.
On either hand a dense and leafy shade,
Silent as death the thick-wove branches made ;
While to our ears the torrent's deadened roar,
Heard through the stillness, seemed to still it more :
Here—so the fancy crossed me as I stood—
Some hermit should be blessed in solitude ;
Here the light song of birds must seldom come,
Here the brisk squirrel would not choose his home,
Flowers bloom not here, but Nature's wildest mood
Speaks from the hoary rocks, the dusky flood.
Yet over all so strange a charm is thrown
(One that abides when brighter charms are flown),
You well might deem the spirit of the place,
Disdaining Summer's loveliness and grace,
Chose this secluded spot to show her power,
And bade it please alike in every hour.
What consolation save the highest, best
Has such a charm to cheer the harassed breast,
As Nature's silent sympathy bestows,
Glad in our pleasure, mournful in our woes ?

There is a mood when every heart-pulse thrills,
And one full chord of joy our being fills,
When happiness, a deep and waveless tide,
Pours through our life and covers all beside—
For such a mood the bounteous mother still
Can add fresh charms to mountain, lawn, or rill ;
Until we dream each newly opened flower
Has donned its bridal garment for that hour.
But far from this, as are the moans of pain
From the glad music of an angel's strain,
There comes a time when, torn and bleeding yet,
The tortured heart has still to learn regret,
Fierce pain uprising drowns sad reason's plea,
And passion cries, " This suffering shall not be ! "
Oh ! in such moments when no mortal nigh
Reads the wild misery in the tearless eye,
And when no human voice, however dear,
May dare to break upon the conflict drear,
Then the deep gorge, the ever-flowing stream,
The cloud-flecked heavens, calm as an infant's dream,
Have subtler ways to reach the troubled heart
Than man's most boasted wisdom can impart,
And softening still as still their charms increase,
The pain grows less, and yields almost to peace.

PART III.

Now the calm beauty of the twilight fades,
And night comes stealing from the denser shades,
The gleaming lights from yonder dwelling far
Scarce twinkle brighter than the first pale star.
Deep mid its green recess the river twines,
And faintly bright through clustering branches shines,
Here the white road goes winding o'er the hill,
In gathering darkness glimmering whitely still.
It is an hour when Fancy well might claim
The mind untrammelled as her just domain,
But not her fairest visions could pourtray
More loveliness than we have seen to-day :
From each tall tree upon the river side
A length'ning shadow crept across the tide ;
While the steep bank in softened verdure lay,
And o'er its summit poured the evening ray,
Shone on wide, fertile fields before us spread,
And crowned with gold each forest monarch's head ;
Round the curved bank the stream embracing flowed,
And as it passed a thousand charms bestowed,
Smiled to the lofty hill, the placid sky,
Kissed the drooped boughs and softly floated by.
Delightful Mohawk ! where thy grassy breast

Woos the pleased stranger's eye to lingering rest,
How calm thy shaded dwellings seem to lie
Abodes of peace and fair tranquillity.
There cheerful and content in rustic toil
We saw the dark-eyed children of the soil ;
Amid their homes the sanctuary stood—
Sign of the faith that knows no alien blood—
And round its walls full many a turfy heap
Breaks into flowers above an Indian's sleep ;
There as we wandered in the solemn shade
We paused awhile where gallant Brant is laid.
Well may he rest !   Around, his people still
Own the broad woods, the spreading farm lands till,
And when the peaceful day of rest draws near
From those old walls is wafted sweet and clear,
In his own tongue, now tuned to Christian lays,
The Indian's Heaven-sent voice of prayer and praise.

PART IV.

If thou dost love the woods, and hold'st it dear
To trace their changing beauties through the year,
From the first day when swelling buds begin
To usher Spring and all her blossoms in,
To the bright hours when Winter's frosty sky

Smiles o'er the leafless branches, cold and high,
And every slender twig its armour wears
Glittering and bright of Autumn's frozen tears,
Thou know'st the silence that will sometimes fall
Mid the bright Summer daylight over all ;
When birds to shelter flying cease their strain,
And breezes hold their breath before the rain,
Light leaves that wont their revels still to keep
From dawn till dusk, now sink at once to sleep,
Bound by a spell they want the skill to break,
Till the shower bids them with a kiss "Awake ! "
Then as they gleam and sparkle, gently stirred,
Again the twittering notes of birds are heard,
No loud, continuous song, but now and then
A carol just commenced and hushed again,
As if the joyous songsters had not power
To utter all the gladness of the hour.
At such a time, deep hidden in the shade,
Methought the flowers a tiny chorus made,
Or else some wand'ring fairy tuned the lay,
Light as the air and gladsome as the day :

    Oh ! the rain, the beautiful rain,
      The rain of the Summer-time,
    Plashing down from the clouded sky
      With a sound like murmured rhyme ;

Dashing against the emerald leaves
  And leaving them glittering wet,
Like a dreaming child, who smiles in his sleep,
  With a tear on his lashes yet.

Oh ! the shadowy, sheltered spots
  In the heart of the forest old,
Where the earliest wildflowers bud and bloom,
  And 'tis late ere they die of cold.
How softly the Summer raindrops fall,
  Distilled through the arches green ;
And you know next day by the fresher bloom
  How welcome the shower has been.

PART V.

Yon diamond-crested waves, methinks, have given
Their freshness to the balmy breath of Heaven,
As on the pebbly beach they brightly play
With murmured song the livelong Summer day.
Here, scarcely seen, just flashing through the shade,
By scattered trees upon the margin made,
Their sunny ripples lend a lovelier grace
To the secluded beauty of the place.

Oh, perfect Nature ! thus to hear and see,
To feel the beauties that attend on thee,
This is a boon that all alike may share,
Free as the flowing tide, th' encircling air.
Th' enchantress Art for some may spread her store,
To others, Wisdom yields her costly lore ;
To some Ambition's glittering prizes fall,
Wealth, Honour, Health, and Love are not for all;
Thou greet'st alone, with equal aspect mild,
Earth's greatest monarch or the cotter's child.

Here, in such scene as this at Summer noon,
Lulled by the buzzing insects' drowsy tune,
Some errant knight might in his wand'rings rest,
Some dauntless champion on the Holy Quest—
But no ! the days of chivalry are gone,
No gleam of armour here has ever shone,
The lovely visions of an earlier time
Lend no enchantment to this late-found clime.
Here cold Reality proclaims her sway,
And Fancy's fair creations shrink away.
But even so—from yonder flickering screen,
Where the young oak-leaves spread their golden green,
The sun looks down through many pleasant hours
On velvet turf enamelled o'er with flowers,

And paints, where round the boughs its tendrils twine,
The purple clusters of the fruitful vine.
Here the soft wandering air that floats along
Sometimes comes laden with the breath of song ;
Unseen the singer, lightly floats the strain,
And rippling waves give back the sweet refrain :

Breath of the Summer flowers !
    Laden with odours sweet,
Gather thy richest stores
    And bear them to her feet.
Fly to the woodland dells,
    Shy violets nestle there ;
And seek in sheltered bounds
    The roses' perfume rare.

Yet bid her, as she breathes
    Thy incense floating by,
Remember every bloom
    Must fade 'neath Autumn's sky.
Then, when thy tale is done,
    Low whisper in her ear :
True Love's the only flower
    That blossoms all the year.

THE LAST EVENING.

Eve after eve the Summer through
  Our boat had floated down the stream :
Eve after eve the river knew
  Our oars' soft plash and silvery gleam.

And now, when Autumn chills grew nigh,
  Day's latest and most glorious hour
In rosy splendours from the sky
  Bathed grassy slope and regal tower.

Soft breathed the air : the river slept :
  The fulness of the year had come ;
A sense of languid sweetness crept
  Upon us, as we drew towards home.

At last one spoke—" We near the shore ;
  Row slowly now.   Whate'er betide,
This hour can come to us no more ;
  Life bears us on."   He spoke and sighed.

That hour is past ; the silent stream
  Bears other boats upon their way;
But we and ours are like a dream
  That faded in the Autumn day.

Parting, and change, and death ! We read
    No dark previsions on that sky ;
No shrouded griefs with silent tread
    Upon the waters passed us by.

And yet not God Himself could call
    That bright day from the vanished past,
Nor gather up the links, whose fall
    Has made that evening hour the last.

www.ingramcontent.com/pod-product-compliance
Lightning Source LLC
Chambersburg PA
CBHW032016010726
47493CB00007B/2436